Vampires
COLORING BOOK · MARTY NOBLE

DOVER PUBLICATIONS, INC.

Mineola, New York

NOTE

The subject of myth, folklore, and romance, the vampire is as fascinating today as it was in 1897 when Bram Stoker's *Dracula* was first introduced. These charismatic, seductive creatures of the night have a fear of death and the desire to be immortal. They drink the blood of their victims to get a rush of power and to survive. Powerful and sexy vampires steal bites from unsuspecting victims as they search for the perfect soul mate to spend eternity with. Here we have a variety of scenes that include bloodthirsty vampires (male and female), castles, bats, a cemetery, and more ready for you to color and bring to life.

Bibliographical Note

Vampires Coloring Book is a new work, first published by
Dover Publications, Inc., in 2010.

International Standard Book Number

ISBN-13: 978-0-486-47848-7
ISBN-10: 0-486-47848-3

Manufactured in the United States by RR Donnelley
47848305   2015
www.doverpublications.com